chicken soup by heart

by Esther Hershenhorn

illustrations by Rosanne Litzinger

Simon & Schuster Books for Young Readers

New York London Toronto Sydney Singapore

SIMON & SCHUSTER BOOKS FOR YOUNG READERS

An imprint of Simon & Schuster Children's Publishing Division

1230 Avenue of the Americas, New York, New York 10020

Text copyright © 2002 by Esther Hershenhorn

Illustrations copyright © 2002 by Rosanne Litzinger

SIMON & SCHUSTER BOOKS FOR YOUNG READERS is a trademark of Simon & Schuster.

Book design by Daniel Roode

The text of this book is set in Aunt Mildred.

The illustrations are rendered in gouache, watercolor,

and colored pencil on fine 140-pound Italian watercolor paper.

Printed in Hong Kong

2 4 6 8 10 9 7 5 3 1

Library of Congress Cataloging-in-Publication Data

Hershenhorn, Esther.

Chicken soup by heart / by Esther Hershenhorn ; illustrated by Rosanne Litzinger.—1st ed.

p. cm.

Summary: When Rudie's sitter gets the flu, he uses her recipe to make her a batch of

special chicken soup, including the secret recipe of stories from the heart.

ISBN 0-689-82665-6

[1. Babysitters—Fiction. 2. Soups—Fiction. 3. Sick—Fiction. 4. Jews—Fiction.]

I. Litzinger, Rosanne, ill. II. Title.

PZ7.H432425 CH 2001

[E]-dc21

00-045067

To my Philadelphia family and their families, too:

my mother and father, Vivian and Samuel Chairnoff,

my sister, Judith Chairnoff Richards, and my brother, Hugh

—E. H.

As the saying goes: Only the pure of heart can make a good soup.

—R. L.

Here it is from start to finish: how such a nice *boychik* saved
the Chicken Soup Queen.

It was a very nice Sunday in the middle of spring, in the middle of breakfast, in the middle of the morning. Rudie Dinkins heard his mama say that Rudie's sitter, Mrs. Gittel, had the flu.

Rudie ran down the hallway to Mrs. Gittel's apartment. He heard thirteen *A-choos!* before he ever *k-nocked*.

"It's me!" Rudie shouted. "My mama says you're sick!"

Mrs. Gittel sneezed again, then blew her nose twice.

She whispered through the door, "*Oy!* You can't come in, Rudie."

Rudie Dinkins had some Very Big Worries now. So big, in fact, he had to sit down to think about them.

"What if it was me who made Mrs. Gittel sick?" he asked. Only last week he'd had a Rudie Dinkins Chest Cold.

"Who will snug-a-bug her like she snug-a-bugged me? Who will cook her chicken soup and make her good as new?"

There was also some supposing as to when she'd be all better. Mrs. Gittel baby-sat him Mondays after school.

Rudie *k-nocked* again.

"Don't worry!" Rudie shouted. "I'm cooking you chicken soup.

You'll be good as new tonight."

In a minute Rudie stood in the middle of his kitchen. This was no small task cooking Mrs. Gittel chicken soup. Mrs. Gittel was the Chicken Soup Queen. She deserved the very best, namely, soup the way *she* cooked it.

Lucky thing! After all his chest colds, Rudie knew her recipe, give or take an ingredient.

Another lucky thing! He knew Mrs. Gittel's chicken soup secret! She stirred in very nice stories about her soon-to-be soup-eaters.

Rudie grabbed his mama and his mama grabbed a soup pot.
Together they filled it so-high with water.

Into the pot went some chicken and a chicken wing, plus
a very nice wishbone Rudie'd saved for Mrs. Gittel.

Of course, leave it to him to sneak in a Rudie Dinkins Surprise!

Guess who knew his sitter liked her soup a little sweet?

This is the first Mrs. Gittel story Rudie stirred in, his mama
nearby just in case her *boychik* spilled.

It was all about the time maybe three months back when he happened to have a Rudie Dinkins Chest Cold. Mrs. Gittel baby-sat him, and like always, made him chicken soup. It was Number Day at school, though. He was very sad to miss it. So while the soup cooked they practiced counting like accountants!

They counted soupspoons and soup nuts and cousins in the picture frames, then love-seat flowers and cowboys on his quilt. Next chin hairs and liver spots and beauty marks and freckles. Every ten numbers they would share a candy Kiss. When they were done they'd counted almost to a thousand!

Mrs. Gittel told him, "You're a regular genius!"

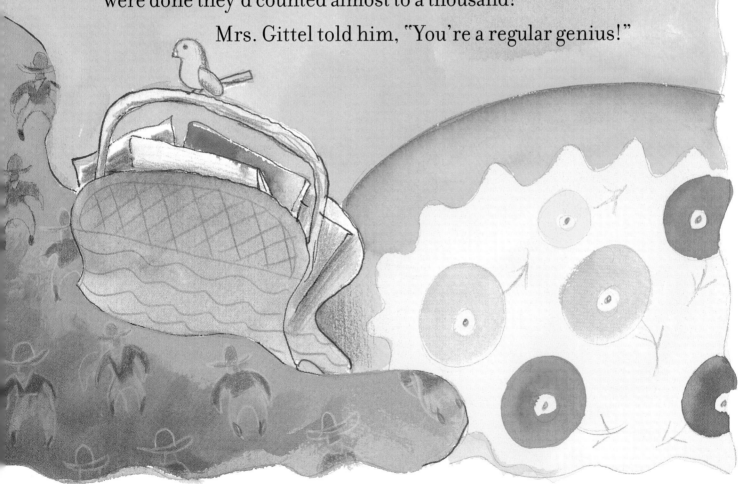

Which was certainly the truth. Only such a smart *boychik* could shoo Mrs. Gittel's flu bug. Rudie brought his chest-cold cream to Mrs. Gittel's door.

"It's me!" Rudie shouted. He *k-nocked* again. "How are you?"

Mrs. Gittel *Oy-oy-oy*-ed! "Don't ask, Rudie."

So in less than a minute Rudie was back in the middle of his kitchen cooking Mrs. Gittel chicken soup.

Rudie added carrots and a little bit of celery, chopped by his mama into very nice chunks.

And leave it to him to sneak in *another* Rudie Surprise! Guess who knew his sitter liked her soup a little sweet?

This is the second Mrs. Gittel story Rudie stirred in.

It was all about the time he stopped by Mrs. Gittel's apartment to give her a look at his brand-new wagon. It was Mrs. Gittel's card-game day. Her fingers hurt like crazy. Mrs. Gittel asked him could he stay and give a help.

So Rudie helped shuffle and Rudie helped deal and Rudie picked a card whenever Mrs. Gittel's turn came. The two of them would whisper, rearranging their cards. Rudie's job was shouting, "Gin! We win!"

Every jelly bean in the candy dish was Rudie's.

Mrs. Gittel told him, "They should bottle you like medicine!"

Which was also the truth. Only such a helpful boy would know which pocket had his cough drops. Rudie wrapped up two to bring to Mrs. Gittel's door.

"It's me!" Rudie shouted. He *k-nocked* again. "How are you?"

Mrs. Gittel *Ei-ei-ei*-ed! "I'm too sick to *Oy!*"

It took twenty seconds tops for Rudie to get back to the middle of his kitchen to finish making chicken soup.

Rudie held his nose while his mama peeled an onion and chopped nice chunks for Rudie to add.

Leave it to him to sneak in one last Surprise! Guess who knew his sitter liked her soup a little sweet?

This is the last Mrs. Gittel story Rudie stirred in.

It was all about the time when Rudie's mama worked a Saturday and Mrs. Gittel's Arthur moved too far away to visit. Rudie and Mrs. Gittel couldn't make a smile no-how, so they walked up the avenue to have themselves a good time.

They watched a parade and posed for pictures in a picture booth, and Mrs. Gittel told him, "You're movie-star handsome!"

Then they stopped and had a bite and *schmoozed* with Mrs. Gittel's girlfriends and Rudie told Mrs. Gittel, "You should have your own talk show!"

Later they were so pooped that they had to rest their tootsies. Mrs. Gittel hugged him.

"We're some very good friends."

Truer words a person never spoke.

Right then Rudie grabbed those pictures, Mama loaded up his wagon, and he wheeled his chicken soup to Mrs. Gittel's door.

"It's me!" he shouted. He *k-nocked, k-nocked, k-nocked.*
"I made you chicken soup with three Mrs. Gittel stories!
Mama said you should cook it up hot. How are you, anyway?"

"You don't want to know!"

Well, what a person wouldn't want to know is how Rudie slept
that night. He had such crazy nightmares in the middle of his head.
All a person needs to know is how Rudie woke up, with a hurt
in his middle and a *k-nock* at the door.

Rudie gave a listen.

"Where's our favorite *boychik?*"

Rudie gave a peek.

"Mrs. Gittel!" he shouted. "My chicken soup worked!"

"You knew my recipe by heart! Plus, leave it to you to make it Rudie Dinkins sweet!"

"*Ooooo!*" Rudie moaned. "*Ooooo! Ooooo! Ooooo!*"

"*Oy!*" said Mrs. Gittel. "That's a Rudie Dinkins Tummy-ache!"

So Mrs. Gittel baby-sat him and snug-a-bugged him tight and
in the middle of the morning fixed him a seltzer.

They played a little cards and they talked and looked at pictures.

Then they made chicken soup to have for supper later.

The two of them together stirred in such a nice story.

"Here it is," she said,
"from start to finish:
how such a nice *boychik* saved
the Chicken Soup Queen. . . ."

RUDIE DINKINS'S CHICKEN SOUP RECIPE

* Fill a big pot so-high with water.
* Put in some chicken.
* Put in some cut-up carrots and a little bit of celery.
* Put in some chunks of onion.
* Stir in three soup-eater stories.
* Cook everything up hot.

MRS. GITTEL'S CHICKEN SOUP RECIPE

* Wash a nice fresh chicken (maybe 6 pounds or so) and then put it in a big soup pot.

* Cover the chicken all over with cold water—maybe 10 or 12 cups worth.

* Heat the water until it bubbles and boils.

* Turn the heat down and cook it some more. Make sure that what you hear is a nice ripple sound, like the soup is smiling from somewhere down deep.

* Meanwhile, use a nice flat spoon, or even a metal one with slots, and take away the foam that keeps coming to the top.

* Throw in 2 large carrots (scraped is a good idea), 2 whole celery stalks, some parsley, some dill, an onion, a leek, some parsnip, a turnip, celery root's nice, and so is some parsley root, and just to stay healthy, put in some garlic, and maybe some peppercorns, and maybe a bay leaf.

* Add salt and pepper until you're happy with the taste.

* Add a pinch of sugar, to make sure it's sweet.

* Cook on the stove at least 3 hours and keep adding water, so the chicken has a cover.

* Then pour out the soup through a sieve or a cheesecloth, so it loses its fat and not-nice parts.

* Then put the soup back and finish up with noodles or matzoh balls or rice or even some dumplings.

* And **remember**: Stir in three very nice stories about your soon-to-be soup-eater!